I Wonder About WORLDS

Discovering Planets and Exoplanets

Written by
James Gladstone

Illustrated by
Yaara Eshet

Owlkids Books

Our SOLAR SYSTEM is made up of the Sun and all the objects that orbit it: planets, dwarf planets, moons, comets, and asteroids.

Eight planets orbit our Sun: Mercury, Venus, Earth, Mars, Jupiter, Saturn, Uranus, and Neptune.

When a solar system object goes around the Sun one time, it's called an orbit. Moons also orbit their planets, just as our Moon orbits Earth.

Mercury, Venus, and Mars are **TERRESTRIAL PLANETS**, just like Earth is. They all have rocky, solid surfaces. But these worlds are also different from each other in many ways.

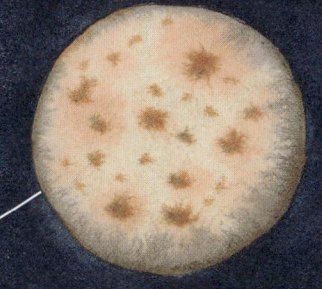

MERCURY is the smallest planet in our solar system. It is also the fastest to orbit the Sun. It speeds through space at close to 106,000 mph (170,000 km/h).

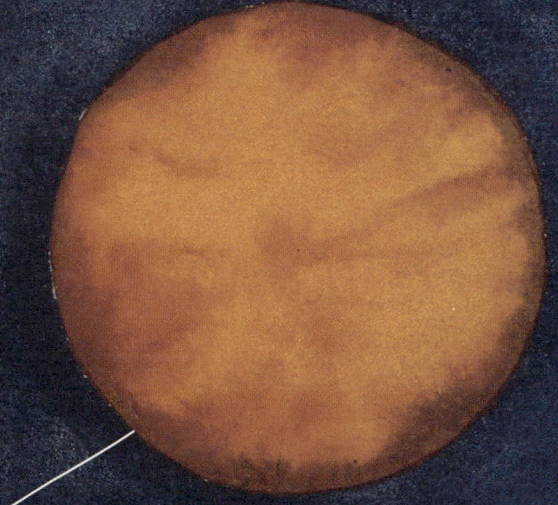

VENUS is hot—the hottest of all the planets in our solar system. Its surface temperature is about 900°F (480°C). Venus is so hot because its atmosphere is full of greenhouse gases that trap heat.

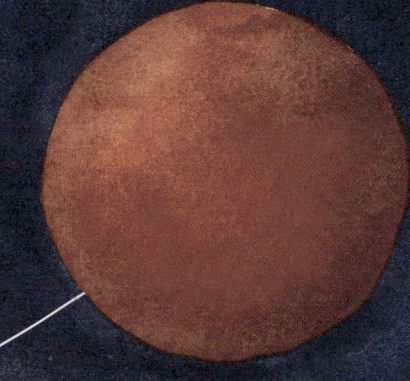

MARS is often called the Red Planet. You can see it as a point of red light in the night sky. Mars gets its color from the iron oxide in its rusty-looking soil.

Jupiter and Saturn are known as GAS GIANTS. They are huge planets made mostly of gases such as hydrogen and helium. But each planet has its own special features.

JUPITER is the biggest planet in the solar system. It's so big that 1,300 Earths could fit inside it.

SATURN is known as the Ringed Planet. Other planets also have rings, but Saturn's rings of ice and rock are the brightest. You can see these rings through a telescope on a clear night.

Other worlds we explore with deep-space probes that send pictures back to Earth.

Like Jupiter and Saturn, the planets Uranus and Neptune have gases in their atmospheres. But astronomers have also learned that these two planets are partly made of stuff called "ices." That's why Uranus and Neptune are known as ICE GIANTS.

URANUS is closer to the Sun's heat than Neptune is, but some of Uranus's atmosphere may be the coldest in our solar system, measured at −371°F (−224°C).

NEPTUNE is the farthest planet from the Sun. Sunlight takes four hours to reach Neptune. A sunny day on Neptune would seem like twilight on Earth.

Some worlds are so far away, we can't
see what they look like at all.

So I rocket through the Milky Way—
a nighttime river of daylight stars ...

Our solar system is part of the MILKY WAY galaxy.
We call it the Milky Way because it looks milky
white in our night sky.

The Milky Way is a spiral galaxy. We can see only
part of our galaxy from Earth because we are inside
of it. If we could travel far outside of the Milky Way,
we could see its whole spiral shape.

The Sun is one star in the Milky Way. There are
billions of other stars in our galaxy. And trillions of
other galaxies fill the whole universe.

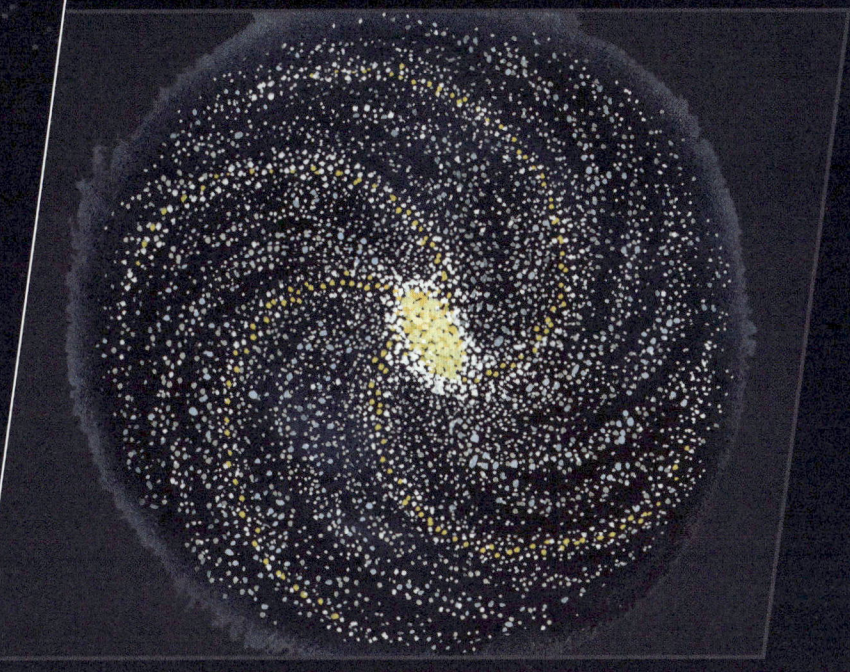

... to see what worlds I can find.

Planets outside of our solar system are called **EXOPLANETS**. They orbit other suns in our galaxy. Astronomers have found thousands of exoplanets, but they think there are billions just waiting to be discovered!

We can't yet see what exoplanets look like because they are so far from Earth. But astronomers have special telescopes to help gather information about these worlds. What they are finding is an incredible variety of exoplanets.

I see a lava world burning fiery hot …

A LAVA WORLD is a type of exoplanet that orbits close to its sun. The temperature is hot on these rocky orbs. Scientists think that a world like this would be partly covered in a red-hot lava ocean.

Some lava worlds are known as super-Earths. A super-Earth is a type of exoplanet that is bigger than Earth but smaller than a giant planet like Neptune.

Other super-Earths may be covered in water or made mostly of gases. Sometimes we call these gassy exoplanets mini-Neptunes.

There may be many more types of super-Earths to discover.

... and a water world with towering waves.

Some **WATER WORLDS** may have watery oceans like Earth. Others may be covered in ice. Still others may have atmospheres filled with water vapor—the gas state of water.

Life on Earth needs liquid water to survive. Scientists wonder if one day they will find signs of life on a water world that has liquid water.

Close up to a burning star,
a hot giant makes its home.

A HOT JUPITER is a gas giant. The planet Jupiter in our solar system is also a gas giant, but with one big difference: our Jupiter is far from our Sun and a hot Jupiter is very close to its sun. And that makes this type of exoplanet blazing hot.

Some hot Jupiters are so close to their suns that they make one orbit in just a few days or less. Compare that to our Jupiter, which takes 4,333 days to orbit the Sun!

And far out from the heat and light,
a cold giant roams with its moons.

> Early in their search for exoplanets, astronomers found lots of gas giants close to their suns. Now they are learning that the Milky Way is also filled with gas giant and ice giant planets that orbit farther out from their stars.

But when I land on a rocky world a bit like planet Earth, I see no people there at all.

TERRESTRIAL EXOPLANETS are rocky worlds. Like the terrestrial planets in our solar system, these rocky exoplanets take different forms. Some may be much hotter or colder than Earth. Some may be the same size as Earth, while others are a bit bigger or smaller. Some may even have liquid water.

The HABITABLE ZONE is a region around a star where the temperature is not too hot and not too cold. This zone is just right for water to remain liquid on a planet.

Earth lies in the habitable zone of our solar system. It is the only world we know of—so far!—that has life.

Astronomers think there may be millions, or perhaps billions, of rocky exoplanets in habitable zones. Is there life on one of these worlds? And could life exist on worlds that are not in habitable zones? Only time and careful study will tell.

That's when I know it's time to turn my ship around and travel straight for home.

Because I want to see my Sun again and my Moon ...

MORE ABOUT THE SOLAR SYSTEM

THE SUN — Our Sun is the center of the solar system. It is a yellow dwarf star, and it's more than 4.5 billion years old. This huge, hot ball of gas is the biggest object in our solar system. More than one million Earths could fit inside it.

The Sun's heat and light energy come from its core. The temperature there is about 27,000,000°F (15,000,000°C). Life on Earth could not exist without energy from the Sun.

Earth is about 93,000,000 mi. (150,000,000 km) from our star. It takes sunlight about eight minutes to travel from the Sun to Earth, but it would take more than 175 years to drive that distance in a car.

MERCURY — This world is covered in craters, large and small bowl-shaped holes caused by comets and meteoroids that have crashed into it. These impact craters make the surface of Mercury look similar to the surface of our Moon. And Mercury is only a bit larger than our Moon.

VENUS — Venus is covered in a thick layer of yellowish clouds. By using radar to see through these clouds, we know that Venus has hundreds of huge volcanoes and thousands of smaller ones. Scientists are trying to find out if any of these volcanoes are still active.

EARTH — Liquid water covers about 70 percent of Earth's surface. That makes Earth both a rocky planet and a water world. Earth's atmosphere is rich in oxygen—a gas we need to breathe. The atmosphere also protects us from much of the Sun's harmful radiation. And Earth is the only planet that has a single moon in its sky. The Moon orbits our planet once about every twenty-seven days.

THE MOON — The Moon is a rocky and dusty place, covered in craters. For millions of years, comets, asteroids, and meteoroids made these craters by crashing into the Moon's surface. When the Moon was young, some impacts made cracks in the thinner areas of the Moon's crust. Lava from within the Moon spilled out of these cracks onto its surface, making lava plains.

The Moon does not make its own light. Moonlight is the Sun's light reflecting off the Moon. When the Sun's light reaches the Moon's surface, temperatures can get up to a scorching 260°F (127°C). But where it is dark, it can be as cold as −280°F (−173°C). That is much hotter and colder than anywhere on Earth.

MARS — Mars is a cold, rocky, and dusty place covered with craters and canyons. Valles Marineris is a system of canyons more than 3,000 mi. (4,800 km) long. Mars also has the tallest volcano in the solar system—Olympus Mons. It's three times higher than Mount Everest on Earth—and Everest is more than 5 mi. (8 km) high. The volcano is quiet now, but scientists think it is possible that lava could flow from it again in the future.

JUPITER — Jupiter has no hard surface to stand on. Scientists are still investigating whether this gas giant has a solid core or a hot, thick soup of iron and minerals at its center. And hurricane-like storms howl through Jupiter's atmosphere. The Great Red Spot is the biggest storm of all. It is bigger than Earth and has been observed since the 1600s. Jupiter also has dozens of moons. One of them, called Ganymede, is the largest moon in the solar system.

SATURN — Saturn is the second-largest planet in the solar system. Like Jupiter, it has huge storms in its atmosphere. Winds can whip close to 1,100 mph (1,800 km/h). Saturn also has dozens of moons. Its biggest moon, Titan, is a huge world, larger than the planet Mercury. And on the moon Enceladus, jets of ice particles and gas rise up from its surface at about 800 mph (1,300 km/h)!

URANUS — Uranus's blue color comes from methane gas in its atmosphere. And each Uranus year is the same as eighty-four Earth years. For about half of Uranus's year, its north pole is bathed in sunlight, while its south pole is in darkness. Then it switches. For the next forty-two years, Uranus's south pole is lit by the Sun.

NEPTUNE — Winds on Neptune reach speeds of more than 1,200 mph (1,900 km/h). That's faster than on any other planet in the solar system. Like Uranus, Neptune gets its blue color from methane in its atmosphere. But Neptune is a deeper blue. Some scientists think this is because Neptune's active atmosphere churns up more methane than that of Uranus, which makes Neptune's atmosphere less hazy and bluer looking.

OTHER SOLAR SYSTEM OBJECTS — There are many other solar system objects you can also find out about: dwarf planets, asteroids, meteoroids, comets, plus all the spacecraft and telescopes people have sent up into space!

What do you wonder about the solar system and the Milky Way? Most of all, what do you wonder about worlds?

*For everyone who had a hand in making this book
and getting it out to our world* — J.G.

*To Nancy Tapley, for showing us the wonders
of the night sky* — Y.E.

The author also thanks Paul A. Delaney, Professor Emeritus, Department of Physics and Astronomy, York University, Toronto. Thank you, Paul, for your time, feedback, and helpful insights. And special thanks to Yaara Eshet for the wonderful and whimsical worlds you imagined for our book!

Text © 2024 James Gladstone | Illustrations © 2024 Yaara Eshet

All rights reserved. No part of this publication may be reproduced, stored in a retrieval system, or transmitted in any form or by any means, without the prior written permission of Owlkids Books Inc., or in the case of photocopying or other reprographic copying, a license from the Canadian Copyright Licensing Agency (Access Copyright). For an Access Copyright license, visit www.accesscopyright.ca or call toll-free to 1-800-893-5777.

Owlkids Books acknowledges the financial support of the Canada Council for the Arts, the Ontario Arts Council, the Government of Canada through the Canada Book Fund (CBF) and the Government of Ontario through the Ontario Creates Book Initiative for our publishing activities.

Owlkids Books gratefully acknowledges that our office in Toronto is located on the traditional territory of many nations, including the Mississaugas of the Credit, the Chippewa, the Wendat, the Anishinaabeg, and the Haudenosaunee Peoples.

Published in Canada by Owlkids Books Inc.,
1 Eglinton Avenue East, Toronto, ON M4P 3A1

Published in the US by Owlkids Books Inc.,
1700 Fourth Street, Berkeley, CA 94710

Library of Congress Control Number: 2023948779

Library and Archives Canada Cataloguing in Publication
Title: I wonder about worlds : discovering planets and exoplanets / written by James Gladstone ; illustrated by Yaara Eshet.
Names: Gladstone, James, 1969– author. | Eshet, Yaara (Illustrator), illustrator.
Identifiers: Canadiana (print) 20230566812 | Canadiana (ebook) 20230566820 | ISBN 9781771475723 (hardcover) | ISBN 9781771476973 (EPUB)
Subjects: LCSH: Extrasolar planets—Juvenile literature. | LCSH: Planets—Juvenile literature. | LCGFT: Informational works. | LCGFT: Picture books.
Classification: LCC QB820 .G53 2024 | DDC j523.2/4—dc23

Edited by Jennifer Stokes and Stacey Roderick | Designed by Alisa Baldwin

Manufactured in Guangdong Province, Dongguan City, China, in March 2024, by Toppan Leefung Packaging & Printing (Dongguan) Co., Ltd.
Job #BAYDC134

hc   A   B   C   D   E   F

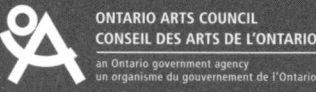

Publisher of Chirp, Chickadee and OWL
www.owlkidsbooks.com

Owlkids Books is a division of bayard canada